Waldo and the Desert Island Adventure

Written and illustrated by
Hans Wilhelm

HAPPY HOUSE BOOKS
Random House, Inc.

Copyright © 1986 by Hans Wilhelm, Inc. All rights reserved under International and Pan-American Copyright Conventions. Published in the United States by Random House, Inc., New York, and simultaneously in Canada by Random House of Canada Limited, Toronto. ISBN: 0-394-87979-1
Manufactured in the United States of America   1 2 3 4 5 6 7 8 9 0

It was raining on Michael's last day of vacation.
He wanted to play on the beach one more time.
But the rain didn't stop.

Michael thought it would be crazy to go out into the rain. But Waldo seemed to think differently.

No one else was outside. They had the whole beach to themselves.

Michael wasn't sure if he would enjoy the walk
in this wet weather.

But after jumping in a few puddles,
Michael forgot all about the rain. They both
found some driftwood.

"Where do you think it came from?" asked
Michael. "Maybe a huge bird flew by and
dropped it on its way to build a nest."

Michael and Waldo sat down and thought
about what fun it would be to have an adventure.
"What if there *was* a huge bird—a really huge
bird—and it saw us and . . ."

Suddenly Waldo and Michael heard loud
squawking above them. "Look out!" shouted
Michael. "It's going to get us!" A huge bird dived
down to attack—when all at once a sea monster
came out of the water and swallowed the bird in
one gulp!

Now the sea monster was
chasing Michael and Waldo! They paddled as fast as they could.

Would they reach the desert island in time?

They had just made it safely to the shore when
Michael spotted some footprints in the sand. "Pirates!"
he cried. "And they've come to bury a treasure!"

"There's their ship!" For Michael and Waldo,
there was no going back. "Attack!" cried Michael,
and both ran toward the pirate ship.

It was a wild battle. But soon the pirates took flight. The ship and the whole island belonged to Michael and Waldo.

They took their time to look at all the treasure left behind by the pirates. But their adventures were not yet over.

Soon they felt hot flames on their backs.
Luckily the brave lion they were riding was
faster than the dragon.

After riding down a huge waterfall, they finally reached safety.

And they were very close to home. Michael and
Waldo decided they had had enough adventures
for the day.

As they soaked in a hot bath with lots of
bubbles, they sang wild pirates' songs together.

And when they were all clean and dry, there was a cup of hot chocolate waiting for each of them.